Cc

is for
California

Written by Carol Greene   Illustrated by Michelle Dorenkamp

Published by GHB Publishers

GHB Publishers, L.L.C.
3906 Old Highway 94 South, Suite 300
St. Charles, MO 63304

Book cover design by Werremeyer |Floresca
Cover illustration by Michelle Dorenkamp

Manufactured in the United States of America
First Edition

10 9 8 7 6 5 4 3 2 1

Library of Congress Cataloging-in-Publication Data

Greene, Carol
C is for California / Carol Greene ; illustrated by Michelle Dorenkamp
Saint Charles, Mo : GHB Publishers, c2000.
p. : ill., maps,
Includes index.

Summary: Presents fascinating facts about California, representing each letter
of the alphabet, from amusement parks to the life zones where
many different plants and animals are located.

English language--Alphabet--Juvenile literature.

California--Juvenile literature.

I. Dorenkamp, Michelle, ill.
II. Title

979.4--dc21   F861.3

ISBN 1-892920-27-1

"A" is for Anaheim • "B" is for Bridge • "C" is for Juan Rodriguez Cabrillo • "D" is for Death Valley • "E" is for Earthquake • "F" is for Fruit • "G" is for Gold • "H" is for Hollywood • "I" is for Imperial Valley • "J" is for Jeans • "K" is for the Kruse Rhododendron Reserve • "L" is for Lake Tahoe • "M" is for John Muir • "N" is for Sierra Nevada • "O" is for the Ocean • "P" is for the La Brea Tar Pits • "Q" is for Quartz • "R" is for Ronald Reagan • "S" is for Junipero Serra • "T" is for Tree • "U" is for the United Nations • "V" is for Volcano • "W" is for Water • "X" is f [Life Zone • "A"] is for Anaheim [Cabrillo • "D" is] for Death Valle [G" is for Gold •] "H" is for Holly ["K" is for the] Kruse Rhododo [for John Muir •] "N" is for Sierra Nevada • "O" is for the Ocean • "P" is for the La Brea Tar Pits • "Q" is for Quartz • "R" is for Ronald Reagan • "S" is for Junipero Serra • "T" is for Tree • "U" is for the United Nations • "V" is for Volcano • "W" is for Water • "X" is for eXtra Facts • "Y" is for Yosemite • "Z" is for Life Zone • "A" is for Anaheim • "B" is for Bridge • "C" is for Juan Rodriguez Cabrillo • "D" is for Death Valley • "E" is for Earthquake • "F" is for Fruit • "G" is for Gold • "H" is for Hollywood • "I" is for Imperial Valley • "J" is for Jeans • "K" is for the

For Nico and Alex Floresca
— C.G.

For my husband, Paul, and my three precious children, Tad, Kate, and Tim
— M.D.

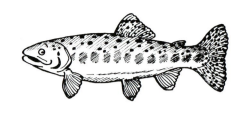

CALIFORNIA STATE SYMBOLS

Animal	California Grizzly Bear
Bird	California Quail
Fish	Golden Trout
Flower	Golden Poppy
Insect	California Dogface Butterfly
Marine Mammal	California Gray Whale
Reptile	Desert Tortoise
Tree	California Redwood

Motto	"Eureka"
Nickname	"Golden State"
Song	"I Love You, California"
State Capital	Sacramento

CALIFORNIA REPUBLIC

CALIFORNIA
history

Native Americans lived in California long before white people came. Spain and England sent the first white explorers in the 1500s.

In 1822, Mexico began to rule California. But more and more people were coming to this beautiful area from the eastern United States. They did not want California to be ruled by Mexico.

The United States and Mexico fought a war that the United States eventually won. In 1850, California became the 31st state.

Meanwhile people poured into California to look for gold. Still more people came to buy land after the Civil War. California was growing fast.

In 1869, the first railroad crossed the Sierra Nevada mountains. In 1915, the new Panama Canal made sea travel easier.

During World War I and World War II, California built factories and shipyards to make war products. In 1963, it became the state with the largest population.

That large population brought problems. California needed more schools, roads, and irrigation. Sometimes different races didn't get along.

But the large population also brought California many gifts. And California gives its people gifts in return.

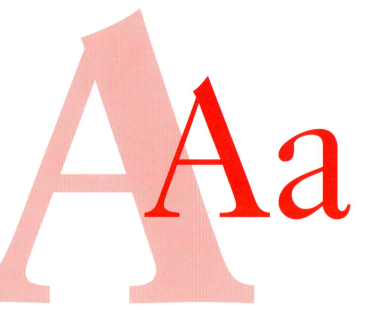

Aa is for Anaheim.

Anaheim

This monument welcomes visitors to the Anaheim Resort.

Millions of tourists visit the city of Anaheim each year.

It is the home of Disneyland, a fantastic amusement park.

There you can meet Mickey Mouse, visit a fairy castle, and enjoy many other adventures.

BBb is for bridge.

Oakland

San Francisco

A ship passes beneath the Golden Gate Bridge.

Two famous bridges cross San Francisco Bay. The beautiful Golden Gate Bridge leads from San Francisco to Marin County. The Oakland Bay Bridge connects San Francisco and Oakland.

Cc is for Juan Rodriguez Cabrillo.

San Diego

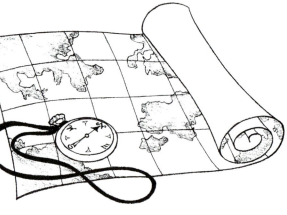

Statue of Juan Rodriguez Cabrillo at the Cabrillo National Monument in San Diego.

In 1542, Juan Rodriguez Cabrillo, a Portuguese explorer, and his men sailed into San Diego Bay. They were the first white men to do this. Cabrillo soon died, but his men sailed north all the way to Oregon.

DDd

is for Death Valley.

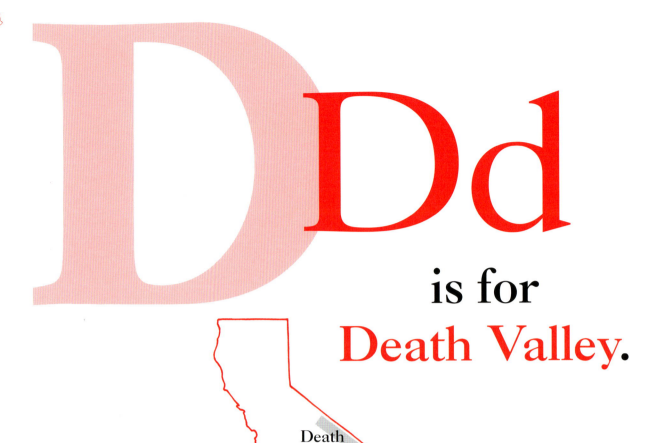

Death Valley

Millions of years ago, Death Valley was an inland sea.

Now it lies 282 feet below sea level, the lowest place in North America.

Death Valley is very hot and very dry.

11

E
Ee

is for **earthquake.**

In 1906,
a terrible
earthquake
hit San
Francisco.

EARTH QUAKE HITS
EVENING NEWS

It started a great fire and shut off all the city's water. Much of San Francisco was destroyed and over 3,000 people died.

Ff is for **fruit.**

Californians grow most of the fruit that people in other states eat.

They grow grapes, apricots, dates, kiwis, nectarines, lemons, melons, peaches, plums, strawberries, oranges — and more!

GGg

is for gold.

Sacramento

In 1848, James Marshall found a small chunk of gold near Sacramento.

Soon thousands of people rushed to California to find gold, too.

17

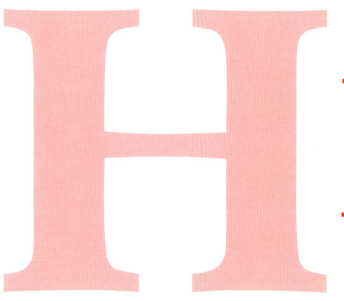

Hh
is for
Hollywood.

Hollywood

DIRECTOR

Action!

In 1911, a company came to Hollywood and filmed a motion picture. Soon Hollywood became the movie capital of the world. Television has taken away some of its power now. But Hollywood still means "movies" to many people.

I Ii is for Imperial Valley.

Imperial Valley

A man fishes in the All-American Canal.

In the middle of southern California lies a desert. In the middle of that desert lies some of the best farmland in the United States. It is called Imperial Valley.

The All-American Canal brings water to the valley from the Colorado River, which is 80 miles away.

J Jj is for jeans.

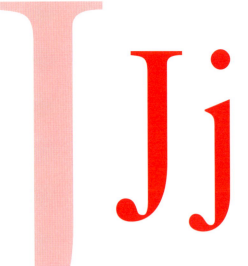

In 1850, Levi Strauss planned to make tents from some heavy cloth he had. A miner asked him to make a pair of work pants instead. They were such good pants that more and more miners wanted them. Jeans (or Levi's) were born.

Kk

is for the **Kruse Rhododendron Reserve.**

• Kruse Reserve

All kinds of beautiful flowers grow in California.

Flowers and seeds are an important business. But many visitors especially like the Kruse Reserve. There rhododendrons grow 20 to 30 feet tall.

L l is for Lake Tahoe.

Lake
Tahoe

26

Glaciers, volcanoes, and earthquakes worked together long ago to form beautiful, deep Lake Tahoe. It lies on the border between California and Nevada. Many people take vacations there.

27

M Mm

is for
John Muir.

Yosemite

John Muir loved nature and wildlife. He wanted others to love and take care of them, too.

Muir started the Sierra Club and helped Yosemite become a national park.

N Nn
is for
Sierra Nevada.

Sierra
Nevada

The Sierra Nevada mountains are in the eastern part of California. The mountains are over 400 miles long and from 40 to 70 miles wide. Visitors marvel at their high peaks and beautiful canyons.

Oo

is for the ocean.

Pacific Ocean

32

The Pacific Ocean splashes along California's western coast for 840 miles. It gives Californians many good gifts: food, transportation, jobs, beautiful sights, and plenty of places to play.

P

Pp is for the La Brea Tar Pits.

Los Angeles

The La Brea Tar Pits in Los Angeles are full of Ice Age fossils.

34

In them, people have found the skeletons of ancient bears, saber-toothed tigers, giant wolves, giant ground sloths, and other prehistoric animals.

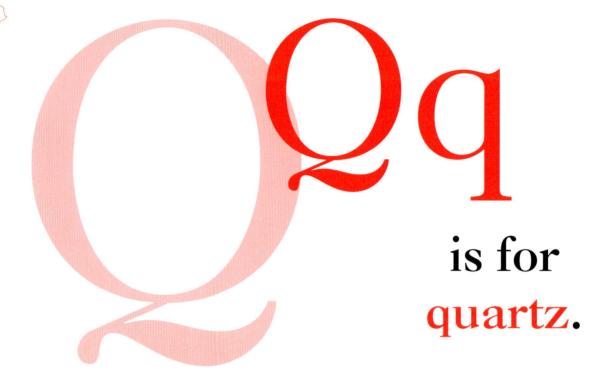

Qq

is for

quartz.

Rose quartz is just one of the lovely gemstones found in California. Other gems include agate, garnet, jade, and tourmaline.

Rr is for Ronald Reagan.

Ronald Reagan was not born in California. But he became famous as a movie actor there.

In 1967, he was elected governor of the state. Then in 1980 and 1984, he was elected president of the United States.

SSs is for Junipero Serra.

Junipero Serra was a Spanish Catholic priest.

In 1769, he built California's first mission at San Diego. Father Serra was a kind man and many people loved him. He became known as the "Father of California."

T t is for tree.

Some amazing trees grow in California.

The bristlecone pines are the oldest living things in the world.

The coastal redwoods are the tallest living things.

U Uu

is for the United Nations.

Members of the United Nations meet in San Francisco on May 8, 1945.

In 1945, representatives from 50 different countries met in San Francisco to sign a paper. The United Nations was born. People hoped it would make the world a better, more peaceful place.

Vv is for volcano.

Lava.
Beds
. Lassen
Peak

A man fly fishes below the backdrop of volcanic Mount Lassen.

Long ago volcanoes helped give California many of its natural features. Lassen Peak in the north is still active. Lava Beds National Monument is a fantasy world of strange shapes.

Ww
is for
water.

The Pacific Ocean gives California plenty of salt water. But dams and other means of irrigation must provide

Water roars from the gates of the Folsom Dam.

enough fresh water to grow California's many crops. Water is important in California!

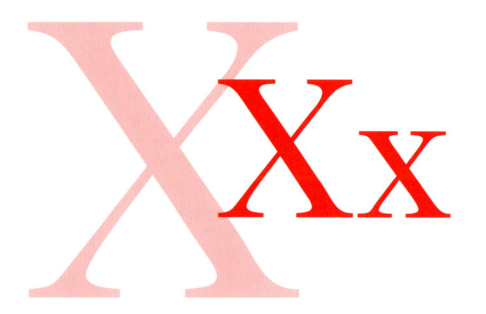

Xx is for eXtra facts.

More people live in California than in any other state in the United States.

California manufactures more goods than any other state. It also grows more crops.

California was probably named after an imaginary treasure island in an old Spanish story.

On July 10, 1913, the temperature in Death Valley climbed to 134 degrees Fahrenheit. That is the hottest temperature ever recorded in the United States.

Y Yy

is for
Yosemite.

Near the center of the Sierra Nevada mountains lies Yosemite National Park. It was named for the Yo Semite Native Americans who lived there. Some people think it is the most beautiful place in the world.

ZZz is for life zone.

A life zone is an area where certain plants and animals can live.

There are seven life zones in North America. California has six of them. That means California has many different plants and animals.

INDEX

SUGGESTED READINGS

Kim Simon, former owner of the children's book wholesaler Reading Express, suggests the following titles to further expand a child's library on California:

Death Valley National Park (A True Book)
Written by David Petersen
Published by Children's Press
Lots of photographs and spare easy-to-read text give a glimpse into what Death Valley is like.

Gold Fever! (A Step into Reading Step 3 Book)
Written by Catherine McMorrow; Illustrated by Mike Eagle
Published by Random House
From the first discovery at Sutter's Mill to the vast influx of prospectors and others out to seek their fortune, here's an anecdotal easy-to-read account that traces the history of the California Gold Rush.

Grandmother Oak
Written by Rosi Dagit; Illustrated by Gretta Allison
Published by Roberts Rinehart
Grandmother Oak has been standing watch on a ridge in Topango State Park for over 200 years — from the time of the Gabrieleno Indians through the Spanish rancheros to today's park visitors. Full color.

Mr. Blue Jeans: A Story About Levi Strauss
Written by Maryann N. Weidt; Illustrated by Lydia M. Anderson
Published by Carolrhoda Books
Traces the life of the immigrant Jewish peddler who went on to found Levi Strauss & Co., the world's first and largest manufacturer of denim jeans.

Yosemite National Park (A New True Book)
Written by David Petersen
Published by Children's Press
Describes the mountains, waterfalls, glaciers, trees, wildlife, and other sights of interest in Yosemite National Park.

REFERENCES FOR TEACHERS/PARENTS

The California Gold Rush: A Guide to the California Gold Rush
Written by Eugene R. Hart
Published by Freewheel Publications

The Complete Guidebook to Yosemite National Park
Written by Steven P. Medley
Published by Yosemite Association

Death Trap: The Story of the La Brea Tar Pits
Written by Sharon Elaine Thompson
Published by Lerner Publications Company

Father Junipero Serra: Founder of California Missions
Written by Donna Genet
Published by Enslow Publishers, Inc.

Plants of the Tahoe Basin: Flowering Plants, Trees and Ferns
Written by Michael Graf
Published by University of California Press

PHOTO ACKNOWLEDGMENTS

Grateful acknowledgment is expressed to the following for permission to reprint their photographs in "C" is for California:

A — Courtesy of the Anaheim Resort.

B — AP/Wide World Photos.

C — Courtesy of the United States Department of the Interior;
National Park Service/Cabrillo National Monument.

D — AP/Wide World Photos.

E — Courtesy of the San Francisco History Center,
San Francisco Public Library.

F — AP/Wide World Photos.

G — Courtesy of the San Francisco History Center,
San Francisco Public Library.

H — AP/Wide World Photos.

I — AP/Wide World Photos.

J — Courtesy of the San Francisco History Center,
San Francisco Public Library.

K — AP/Wide World Photos.

L — AP/Wide World Photos.

M — Courtesy of the San Francisco History Center,
San Francisco Public Library.

N — AP/Wide World Photos.

O — AP/Wide World Photos.

P — AP/Wide World Photos.

Q — Tim Cox.

R — AP/Wide World Photos.

S — Courtesy of the San Francisco History Center,
San Francisco Public Library.

T — AP/Wide World Photos.

U — AP/Wide World Photos.

V — AP/Wide World Photos.

W — AP/Wide World Photos.

Y — AP/Wide World Photos.

Z — AP/Wide World Photos.